# DISNEY
### ◆ PRINCESS

# Forever a Princess

## The stories of
## Cinderella, Belle, & Ariel

retold by Sue Kassirer

**Reader's Digest**
Children's Books™

Pleasantville, New York • Montréal, Québec • Bath, United Kingdom

# Cinderella

## *A Dream Come True*

✦ ✦ ✖ ✦ ✦ ✖ ✦ ✦ ✖ ✦ ✦ ✖ ✦ ✦ ✖ ✦ ✦ ✖ ✦ ✦ ✖ ✦ ✦ ✖ ✦ ✦

Every day was the same. I woke up early, cleaned the house, washed the dishes, mopped the floors, and took care of my Stepmother and two stepsisters.

But someday my dreams would come true. I just knew it. I would wear beautiful gowns and dance at fancy balls. Maybe I would even fall in love!

One day a messenger arrived
with an invitation to a royal ball! I
begged my Stepmother to let me go.
"I see no reason why you can't
go," she said, "*if* you get all your
work done."

As evening fell, I finished all my chores. But, just as I was about to leave for the ball, my stepsisters ruined the gown I was wearing. I ran into the garden and cried.

Suddenly, a Fairy Godmother appeared out of nowhere! She asked me why I was crying, and I told her.

With a wave of her wand, she turned my rags into a beautiful

gown and sent me off to the ball in a glittering coach. But she warned me, "On the twelfth stroke of midnight, the spell will be broken, and everything will be as it was before!"

The minute I walked into the ballroom my eyes and the Prince's met. We danced…and danced… until the clock began to strike midnight.

In haste, I ran down the palace stairs and lost one of my glass slippers.

But it was that slipper that made the magic, for the Prince searched and searched for the one girl whose foot it would fit. And *I* was that girl!

We had a royal wedding. And we lived happily ever after. You see, my dream did come true. I fell in love with a wonderful Prince.

# Belle

## True Love

+ + ✗ + + ✗ + + ✗ + + ✗ + + ✗ + + ✗ + + ✗ + +

As a child, I was not a princess. I was simply Belle, a dreamer and a reader. Books magically swept me away from the small, humdrum village in which I lived. And when I grew older, they saved me from Gaston—a handsome, but oh-so-boring suitor.

Then, one day, my life changed. I had to rescue Papa, who had been imprisoned by a cruel Beast in a castle. A spell had turned him into a Beast. I begged the Beast to take *me* instead of Papa, and although Papa protested, the Beast agreed and let him go.

There I was, the Beast's prisoner. How mean he was—and how scary!

But then…he surprised me. He risked his life to save me from a pack of vicious wolves.

Gradually, we became friends and I grew to enjoy his company. But still, I longed to see Papa. Out of kindness, the Beast let me go. I was free!

But guess what? I missed the Beast and discovered that I cared about him—especially when I heard that Gaston was planning to attack him! I leapt on my horse and got there just in time. I think the sight of me while he was on the rooftop gave the Beast the strength to fight off Gaston....

As the Beast lay there, badly wounded, I wept and said, "I love you," for that was how I felt.

Suddenly, the Beast turned into a
most handsome prince! Looking into his
eyes, I recognized the
gentle and kind person
I had learned to love.

All he needed to break the spell was to learn how to love and to be loved in return. After that, we married and lived happily ever after as prince and princess.

# Ariel

## *Follow Your Dream*

✦ ✦✕✦ ✦✕✦ ✦✕✦ ✦ ✦✕✦ ✦✕✦ ✦✕✦ ✦✕✦ ✦ ✦

All my life I had lived under the beautiful sea. But even as a little girl I was fascinated by the land and by humans. Other than singing, human-watching was my favorite pastime.

I'll never forget the first time I saw him. There I was, peering over the deck of a ship—and Prince Eric appeared. It was love at first sight.

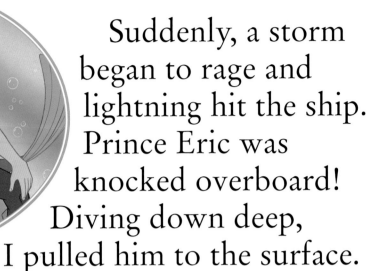

Suddenly, a storm began to rage and lightning hit the ship. Prince Eric was knocked overboard! Diving down deep, I pulled him to the surface. I saved his life!

When my father, King Triton, found out, he was furious. He told me to never go near humans again!

But I was truly lovesick. I went to see Ursula, the sea witch, who offered to turn me into a human. If, in three days, I could get Eric to kiss me, I would remain human. But if he *didn't* kiss me, I would turn back into a mermaid and belong to Ursula forever!

In return, I agreed to give Ursula my beautiful voice. As I sang, my voice flowed into a seashell locket. I could no longer speak.

For three days I tried to get the prince to kiss me. Every day he came closer…and closer. But each time, something went wrong. If only I could talk, or enchant him with my singing!

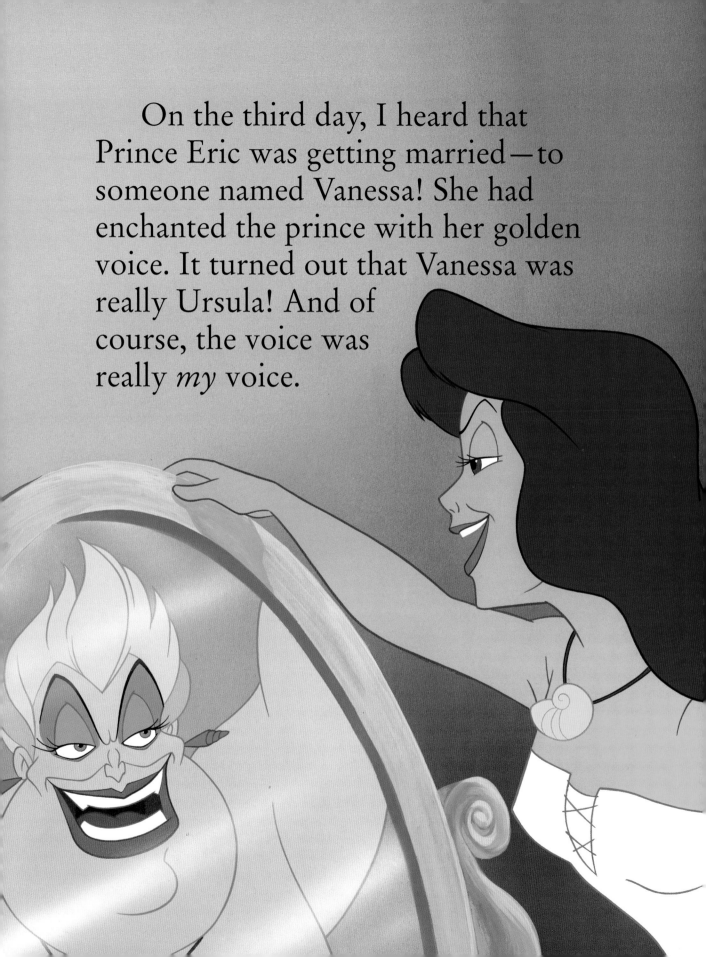

On the third day, I heard that Prince Eric was getting married—to someone named Vanessa! She had enchanted the prince with her golden voice. It turned out that Vanessa was really Ursula! And of course, the voice was really *my* voice.

When all my sea and bird friends heard this, they rushed to the wedding and attacked Vanessa. Her locket crashed to the ground and out flew my voice, which magically returned to me.

When the prince heard me speak,
he knew that it was *me* he loved. From
that day on, we have lived most happily
ever after.

 # How to use this book

Now that you've met Cinderella, Belle, and Ariel, help them look glamorous as they prepare for the royal ball. They are depending on you to make them look dazzling.

- Carefully press out all the dresses and accessories for each princess.

- Now it's time to try some dresses on! Punch out several adhesive dots and stick them on a doll's body and legs. Make sure they are spread out.

- Choose a dress and press it onto the dots so it stays put.

- Are you ready to make the dress even more dazzling? Use the jewels and stickers to make it look extra-special!

- Don't forget the accessories! An elegant outfit is not complete without a pretty necklace, crown, or bouquet of flowers. Use your adhesive dots to attach these to your doll, too.

- To make your doll stand up, assemble the base as shown in figure on right.

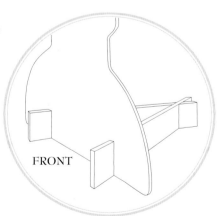

- The adhesive dots are reusable. If they lose their stickiness, you can gently wipe them with a damp towel and allow them to dry.